ACTIVITY ADVENTURE

GROSSET & DUNLAP
Published by the Penguin Group
Penguin Group (USA) Inc., 375 Hudson Street, New York, New York 10014, USA
Penguin Group (Canada), 90 Eglinton Avenue East, Suite 700, Toronto, Ontario M4P 2Y3,
Canada (a division of Pearson Penguin Canada Inc.)
Penguin Books Ltd., 80 Strand, London WC2R ORL, England
Penguin Group Ireland, 25 St. Stephen's Green, Dublin 2, Ireland
(a division of Penguin Books Ltd.)
Penguin Group (Australia), 250 Camberwell Road, Camberwell, Victoria 3124, Australia (a
division of Pearson Australia Group Pty. Ltd.)
Penguin Books India Pvt. Ltd., 11 Community Centre, Panchsheel Park,
New Delhi—110 017, India
Penguin Group (NZ), 67 Apollo Drive, Rosedale, North Shore 0632, New Zealand
(a division of Pearson New Zealand Ltd.)
Penguin Books (South Africa) (Pty.) Ltd., 24 Sturdee Avenue,
Rosebank, Johannesburg 2196, South Africa

Penguin Books Ltd., Registered Offices: 80 Strand, London WC2R ORL, England

ISBN 978-0-448-45599-0   10 9 8 7 6 5 4 3 2

ACTIVITY ADVENTURE

by Katherine Noll
Grosset & Dunlap
An Imprint of Penguin Group (USA) Inc.

INTRODUCTION

Get ready to dive into activities based on your favorite Club Penguin characters, places, and games, which you can do anytime and anywhere.

DELICIOUS RECIPES

Go on a treasure hunt while snacking on yogurt, make snowball cupcakes (but please don't throw them!), or challenge a friend to a *Card-Jitsu* salad.

COOL CRAFTS

Play *Ice Fishing* in your living room, make a magnet of your favorite Club Penguin character, or create your own penguin out of clay.

AWESOME ACTIVITIES

Go on an EPF mission to search for Herbert P. Bear, turn your kitchen into the Pizza Parlor, or practice your acting skills with friends.

POPULAR PUZZLES

Test your Club Penguin knowledge with challenging puzzles and twisty mazes.

WORDS GALORE

Use the Club Penguin clues to fill in crossword puzzles, complete word searches, and create your own silly stories.

BEFORE YOU GET STARTED

For many of the activities, all you need is a pen. The crafts and recipes take some planning ahead, but most use common household items.

Make sure to get a parent's or guardian's permission and help before following any of the recipes or doing any of the crafts.

ASK A PARENT FOR HELP

WHO'S APPEARING ON CLUB PENGUIN?

Penguins all over the island are buzzing. A famous penguin is going to make an appearance on the Iceberg! To find out who it is, follow the instructions below to cross out letters in the grid. The remaining letters will spell out the name of this special penguin.

1 Cross out any letters found in the first part of this crab's name.

Here's a hint: He's Herbert P. Bear's best friend.

3 Cross out any letters that appear in this place's name.

2 Do you know who this penguin is? Cross out any letters found in his first name.

4 Cross out any letters left in column 4.

	1	2	3	4	5	6	7	8
	K	S	D	B	L	O	U	C
	T	Z	Z	G	E	N	Y	K
	R	D	L	M	O	U	C	S
	T	A	E	F	Z	I	Y	R

_____

NAME THAT PLACE

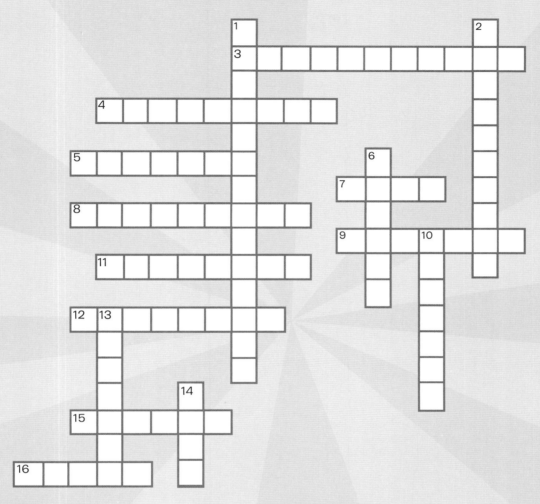

ACROSS

3. Grab a bite to eat here—one of the most popular places on the island.
4. Put your dancing skills to the test here.
5. Sports fans love to play soccer here.
7. Master the elements here.
8. Take a wild ride on a cart at this underground place.
9. Adopt a puffle here.
11. Play *Ice Fishing* in this building.
12. Shop for the latest fashions here.
15. A bright light guides the way to this place.
16. Be a star or enjoy a show here.

DOWN

1. If you have what it takes, you can visit this top secret place.
2. Put on a green apron to serve hot drinks at this place.
6. This outdoor spot has plenty of pine trees to hide behind.
10. What goes up must come down. Head here to hit the icy slopes.
13. Many penguins have tried to tip this spot, but none have succeeded.
14. Have a beach bash or catch some waves here.

LET'S GO *ICE FISHING!*

Make your own game of *Ice Fishing*, then challenge your friends to make the biggest catch of the day.

YOU WILL NEED:

- long sticks or wooden dowels
- string
- small, square magnets
- tape
- paper clips

STEP 1

Tie a piece of string to the end of a stick with a tight knot. Cut the string so that it's long enough to touch the floor when you are standing up.

STEP 2

Attach a magnet to the end of the string with a piece of tape.

STEP 3

Cut out the *Ice Fishing* pieces on page 63. Attach a paper clip to each piece.

STEP 4

Put the pieces in a pile on the floor with the pictures facing up.

Now it's time to play *Ice Fishing*! Players take turns "fishing" with their pole. When they catch one of the *Ice Fishing* pieces with the magnet on the end of their pole, their turn is over. Flip over the piece when caught and follow the instructions. Some pieces earn points, others lose points, and some make you lose a turn!

- Players should keep all of their catches in a pile until the end of the game.

- Players keep taking turns fishing until all the fish are gone.

- Add up the points on the back of the fish to determine the winner.

A BUSY DAY AT THE PIZZA PARLOR SILLY STORY

Fill in the blanks with a friend to come up with your own funny Club Penguin tale!

Hint: A **noun** is a person, place, or thing. An **adjective** is a word that describes something. A **verb** is an action word.

Example:

Head over to the ____Gift Shop____ to buy a/an ____silly____ puffle.
NOUN   ADJECTIVE

One afternoon _____ and _____ decided to go to the Pizza
      YOUR PENGUIN'S NAME   YOUR FRIEND'S PENGUIN'S NAME

Parlor. "I'm so _____, I could eat a _____," _____ said.
      ADJECTIVE   NOUN   YOUR PENGUIN'S NAME

But when they _____ in, they saw the Pizza Parlor was filled with _____
     VERB (PAST TENSE)   ADJECTIVE

_____. There were no empty tables.
ANIMAL (PLURAL)

A _____ came running out of the kitchen. "You must help me," he said. "There are so
   NOUN

many _____ here, I can't make the pizzas fast enough."
    ANIMAL (PLURAL)

The _____ gave _____ to _____ and
     NOUN   ARTICLE OF CLOTHING (PLURAL)   YOUR PENGUIN'S NAME

_____ and walked them into the _____.
YOUR FRIEND'S PENGUIN'S NAME   NOUN

"Put these on and get _____!" he said.
         VERB ENDING IN "ING"

_____ and _____ began making _____.
YOUR PENGUIN'S NAME   YOUR FRIEND'S PENGUIN'S NAME   PLURAL NOUN

First they put on the _____, then the _____, and then some
          NOUN   NOUN

_____. But when they ran out of pizza dough, _____ had to make more.
  NOUN   YOUR PENGUIN'S NAME

"This _____ isn't rising fast enough," _____ said. "Let me add
    NOUN   YOUR FRIEND'S PENGUIN'S NAME

some more _____."
      NOUN

_____ added an entire box of _____ to the pizza dough. The
YOUR FRIEND'S PENGUIN'S NAME   NOUN

dough began to rise. It grew so _____ that it filled the _____.
         ADJECTIVE   NOUN

"_____," yelled _____ as the _____ swept them both out
 EXCLAMATION   YOUR PENGUIN'S NAME   NOUN

of the kitchen and into the dining room.

The _____ who were _____ screamed and ran out of the restaurant.
   ANIMAL (PLURAL)   VERB ENDING IN "ING"

"Hey, guess what?" _____ said to _____. "Now there are
      YOUR PENGUIN'S NAME   YOUR FRIEND'S PENGUIN'S NAME

some empty tables. I think I'll have the _____ _____ pizza."
                      ADJECTIVE   NOUN

PIZZA PARLOR LOGIC PUZZLE

Five penguins are about to order delicious pizzas at the Pizza Parlor. Use the process of elimination to figure out which penguin is ordering which pizza. Carefully read the clues below to find out.

Hint: No two penguins are ordering the same pizza.

1   The green penguin is in the mood for something sweet.
2   The blue penguin and the yellow penguin both like spicy food.
3   The yellow penguin doesn't like shellfish.
4   One of the toppings on the red penguin's pizza is the same color
    as snow.

	SPICY SEAWEED PIZZA	CHOCOLATE SPRINKLE PIZZA	HOT SHRIMP PIZZA	CHEESE PIZZA	MARSHMALLOW PIZZA
BLUE PENGUIN					
YELLOW PENGUIN					
BROWN PENGUIN					
GREEN PENGUIN					
RED PENGUIN					

OPEN YOUR OWN PIZZA PARLOR

There is a lot of work to be done in the Pizza Parlor! Penguins go there to lend a helping flipper as managers, waiters, cashiers, and chefs. Now you can turn your own home into a pizza parlor with these ideas:

PLAN AHEAD

First, ask a parent or guardian for permission! Then ask them when the best time would be to open your restaurant: lunch or dinner?

ASK A PARENT FOR HELP

MAKE YOUR MENU

Your next step is to choose what type of pizza you want to serve. You can use the recipe on page 14 or a favorite recipe of your own. If you don't want to make your pizza from scratch, you could buy frozen pizza to cook and serve. Always ask an adult for permission before cooking!

Don't forget to put drinks on the menu. For a well-rounded menu, add some other dishes, too. Try the *Card-Jitsu* salad on page 34 and the sushi sandwich rolls on page 40.

List all the items that are available for your customers to order on a printed menu. Make sure to have a copy for each customer!

Decide if you're going to charge money. If so, put the prices next to the items.

WORK IT OUT

If you've got a group of people helping you run the restaurant, decide ahead of time which job each person will do. A host or hostess greets the customers and seats them at the table. A waiter takes the customers' orders and brings them their food. The chef cooks the food. Customers pay the cashier for their meal. A manager helps make sure everything is running smoothly and pitches in where needed.

SET THE SCENE

Before you open your Pizza Parlor for business, decorate! Add flowers to a vase or jar for a table centerpiece. Make place mats out of construction paper by cutting a scalloped edge around the paper. Don't forget napkins, knives, and forks for your customers to use.

Set the dining mood with some music! Place a radio or CD player near the dining area to play some tunes that will keep your guests happy.

OPEN FOR BUSINESS

You've created a menu, given out jobs, cooked, and decorated—you're ready to open your Pizza Parlor. After you feed your hungry customers, there is only one thing left to do—clean up! But if your customers really loved their meal, maybe they'll pitch in and help.

PORTRAIT PIZZAS

Get creative in the kitchen by making a pizza that really is a work of art!

YOU WILL NEED:

ASK A PARENT FOR HELP

- English muffins or round sandwich rolls
- mozzarella cheese (sliced or shredded)
- pizza sauce
- toppings (mix and match): green, red, and yellow peppers; pepperonis; carrots; black olives; basil leaves; diced tomatoes; anything else edible you'd like to make art with!

STEP 1

Split open and lightly toast the English muffins or rolls.

STEP 2

Now it's time to make your portrait. Spread the pizza sauce on the muffin and top with cheese. Arrange your toppings to make a face. Get creative!

STEP 3

With an adult's help, place the pizzas in the oven or toaster oven for a few minutes until the cheese melts.

SUGGESTIONS

PENGUIN FACE

Top with sauce and cheese. Add two strips of pepper on the sides of the muffin to make the shape of a penguin head. Use a piece of yellow pepper for the beak. Use two sliced black olives for the eyes and cut a sliced olive in half for the mouth.

RED PUFFLE FACE

Put cheese on the muffin first. Then add the sauce. Cut eyes out of a slice of cheese and place on the muffin. Top with black olives for the pupils.

SILLY FACE

Top with sauce and cheese, then use two slices of carrots for the eyes. Dot the carrots with peppers or another vegetable for the pupils. Cut a triangle out of a pepperoni to use for the nose. Use a strip of pepper in a smiley shape for the mouth. Cut out a small piece of red pepper or pepperoni to make a tongue sticking out.

TIP

For plain pizzas, simply spread sauce on the muffins, top with cheese, and pop in the oven!

GARY THE GADGET GUY'S WORD SCRAMBLE

Gary is Club Penguin's resident inventor. Can you unscramble the names of some of Gary's most famous inventions? Write the answers on the lines. Then write the circled letters in order on the spaces below to find out a secret about Gary.

WORD BANK

JET PACK ADVENTURE

SNOWBALL-POWERED CLOCK

FLARE FLINGER 3000

SPY PHONE

CLOUD MAKER 3000

RECYCLETRON 3000

LIFE PRESERVER SHOOTER

SKI LIFT

FURENSIC ANALYZER 3000

Wonlblsa-Weorped Lckoc   _ _ _ _ _ _ _ _ - _ _ _ _ _ _ _ _

Ifel Vperrrese Seotrho   _ _ _ _ _ _ _ _ _ _ _ _ _ _ _ _

Elceotcryrn 3000   _ _ _ _ _ _ _ _ _ _ 3000

Pys Heonp   _ _ _ _ _ _ _ _

Lfrea Glfienr 3000   _ _ _ _ _ _ _ _ _ _ _ 3000

Cfunreis Alnzyrea 3000   _ _ _ _ _ _ _ _ _ _ _ _ _ _ _ 3000

Isk Filt   _ _ _ _ _ _ _

Culdo Kmrae 3000   _ _ _ _ _ _ _ _ _ 3000

Ejt Capk Vedrauten   _ _ _ _ _ _ _ _ _ _ _ _ _

Besides inventing helpful items to use around the island, Gary also works for the _ _ _ _ _ _ _ _ _ _ _ _ _ _ _ _ _ _ _ _.

MEMORY GAME

Elite Penguin Force Agents need to have excellent observation skills and good memories. Challenge your friends with this EPF Agent game.

YOU WILL NEED:

- tray or table
- towel or small blanket
- paper and pens
- various small objects (such as small toys, pencils/pens, spoons, etc.)

STEP 1

While you are alone, arrange the objects on the tray. Cover the tray with the towel so none of the objects are showing.

STEP 2

Gather your friends around the tray and remove the towel. Count slowly to ten and then cover the tray with the towel again.

STEP 3

Have your friends write down, from memory, all the objects they saw on the table. The person who can name the most objects wins!

If you want to practice your memory skills, ask a friend or family member to set up the game for you.

PENGUIN, PLACE, OR THING?

Can You Guess Who (or What) I Am?

1. You can find me in every room on the island.

2. I can make you laugh.

3. Sometimes I can be puzzling.

4. If anything new is happening on the island, I know about it.

5. I share secrets about Club Penguin with you.

6. I don't cost any coins.

7. I am the "write" place for Aunt Arctic to hang out.

8. You can find out when a new pin will be hidden by checking me out.

Do you know who or what I am?

_____

HIDE-AND-SEEK HERBERT

Members of the Elite Penguin Force are always trying to put a stop to Herbert P. Bear's latest plot. Practice your tracking skills by playing this game, either indoors or outdoors.

- Work together with at least four agents on this field-op.

- Divide everyone into two teams: **ELITE AGENTS** and **HERBERT'S HELPERS**.

- Pick a place to be Herbert's Hideout. It can be anything from a couch to a tree. This will be the base.

- The Elite Agents count while Herbert's Helpers hide.

- The Elite Agents must find all of Herbert's Helpers and tag them before they can make it back to Herbert's Hideout.

- The Elite Agents win if they catch all of Herbert's Helpers.

- Herbert's Helpers win if they get at least one player back to the hideout without being tagged.

- Once the game is over, it's time to switch teams. Elite Agents are now Herbert's Helpers, and Herbert's Helpers are now Elite Agents. Then play again!

TIP

One player from the Elite Agent team should guard Herbert's Hideout.

FOR YOUR EYES ONLY! SPOT THE DIFFERENCES

Only penguins who have what it takes can become Agents in the Elite Penguin Force. If you do become an Agent, you'll receive your orders in the EPF Command Room. Your mission today: These two pictures are not the same. Find and circle the thirteen changes in the picture on the bottom to prove you're Elite Agent material.

FAVORITE THINGS

How well do you know Captain Rockhopper, Sensei, Cadence, Aunt Arctic, and Gary the Gadget Guy? Find and circle their favorite things in the word search below. Remember to search forward, backward, and diagonally. When you're done finding all the words, see if you can match the things to the penguin who likes them best.

```
I F J I I C P G I F L Q O T F S
V N M K O S N I I G K B H A E C
A V V F I I T H N L A T N M C I
B Z F E T G S Y C K O T I H R S
I E Z I N U S A K D H T W Z E U
E D R O S T R W D D N A D Q A M
Q W H T Q D I A C I M E T W M I
L D Q I J B V O U P F S D V S S
E I E I H U C G N B O O M B O X
E R T T M X N G G S D W X W D S
S S U D H E A D P H O N E S A E
U Y I S P R O T A R G I M T N L
P B S B A Y A R R O S K F E C F
T I U A I E U K I A H O T A I F
K L M S U Q R O I O W M Y S N U
C M S N I P M T P I Z Z A N G P
```

WORD BANK

BOOM BOX
CARD-JITSU
CLUB PENGUIN TIMES
COFFEE
CREAM SODA
DANCING
HAIKU

HEADPHONES
INVENTIONS
MIGRATOR
MUSIC
PINK HAT
PINS
PIZZA

PUFFLES
SUSHI
TEA
TREASURE
WRITING
YARR

Match the penguins to their favorite things by writing them on the lines below.

Aunt Arctic

_____ _____ _____ _____

Cadence

_____ _____ _____ _____

Captain Rockhopper

_____ _____ _____ _____

Gary the Gadget Guy

_____ _____ _____ _____

Sensei

_____ _____ _____ _____

MAKE YOUR OWN PIRATE SPYGLASS

Search for treasure and navigate your pirate ship with this spyglass that can actually slide back and forth!

YOU WILL NEED:

- 2 empty paper towel rolls
- tape
- ruler
- markers, paints, glitters, stickers—anything you would like to use to decorate your spyglass
- string
- scissors
- plastic wrap or cellophane

ASK A PARENT FOR HELP

STEP 1

Cut two inches off the length of one of the paper towel rolls. This will be the outer sleeve of your telescope.

STEP 2

Take the other roll and cut the entire roll lengthwise from top to bottom, creating a slit.

STEP 3

Tuck the cut end of the slit under the other end and wrap until the roll is small enough to slide freely in the outer roll. Once you have the desired size, tape the slit closed. This will be the inner piece of your spyglass.

STEP 4

Decorate the rolls.

STEP 5

Cut a piece of string or yarn the same length as the longer, inner piece.

STEP 6

Tape one end of the string to the end of the inner piece.

STEP 7

Place both pieces end to end so the string is overlapping the shorter, outer piece.

STEP 8

Cut the end of the string so that it is two inches shorter than the outer piece.

STEP 9

Tape the other end of the string to the inside of the outer piece.

STEP 10

Cut a piece of plastic wrap to fit the end of the outer piece. Tape it to the same end of the outer piece that you taped the string to. This will be your lens.

Shiver me timbers! Your pirate spyglass is ready for action.

HOW TO HOLD A TREASURE HUNT

You don't need a pirate ship and a parrot to find treasure! You can hold a treasure hunt anytime, anywhere with these easy instructions.

YOU WILL NEED:

- paper
- something to write with
- scissors
- treasure hunters
- treasure—This can be anything you'd like, from candy to a small toy.

STEP 1

Write each of the clues from the next page on a piece of paper. Number each clue.

STEP 2

Cut out each clue.

STEP 3

Hide all of the clues except the first one. Hide clue #2 inside the answer to clue #1 (the freezer). Continue until you reach the answer to the last clue (a towel). Hide the treasure under the towel.

STEP 4

Give the treasure hunters the first clue and let the fun begin!

CLUES

1. It's the coolest spot in the house. FREEZER

2. Potatoes like to sit on this, but not the kind you eat. COUCH

3. It's what you use to visit Club Penguin. COMPUTER

4. You answer it even though it never asks you any questions. TELEPHONE

5. When you turn this off, it is delighted. LAMP

6. Find my tale between two covers. BOOK

7. It has four legs but can't run. TABLE

8. The more it dries, the wetter it gets. TOWEL

TIP
Now that you're a treasure hunt expert, you can make up your own clues for another hunt. Try making one outside!

TREASURE HUNT SURPRISE

Even if the *Migrator* is not docked at the Beach, you can still hunt for treasure in this delicious yogurt cup. Instead of diamonds and jewels, you can dig up (and eat) your favorite berries!

YOU WILL NEED:

- paper or plastic cups
- vanilla yogurt
- blueberries, washed
- strawberries, washed and diced
- graham crackers
- mini umbrellas

ASK A PARENT FOR HELP

STEP 1
Layer some yogurt in the bottom of the cup.

STEP 2
Add a layer of blueberries.

STEP 3
Top with more yogurt.

STEP 4
Top with strawberries.

STEP 5
Add a final layer of yogurt.

STEP 6
Crush up a graham cracker and sprinkle the crumbs on top of the yogurt so it looks like sand.

STEP 7
Decorate with an umbrella and serve!

TIP

Swap out the blueberries and strawberries for your favorite fruits!

BLACK BELT

Both of these penguins are one match away from winning the ultimate *Card-Jitsu* prize: a black belt. Which one will win and become a ninja? Only one penguin's path leads to the black belt.

CARD-JITSU FIRE VOLCANO

Before you begin, be sure you ask an adult to help!

Ninjas were presented with a new challenge when a volcano suddenly appeared near the Dojo, sending lava and smoke into the sky. You can make your own erupting volcano with simple household ingredients such as baking soda and vinegar.

YOU WILL NEED:

For the lava:
- vinegar
- red food coloring
- 1 tbsp baking soda

For the volcano:
- large tray to make the volcano on— one big enough to catch all the lava!
- empty aluminum can (a soup can works well) or plastic cup
- clay

STEP 1

Place your can or plastic cup on the tray.

STEP 2

Form the clay around the can into the shape of a volcano. Make sure to leave the opening of the can clear— this is where the lava will erupt from.

STEP 3

Decorate your tray or volcano as desired (trees, rocks, toys), but remember—everything around the volcano will be covered with lava!

STEP 4

Fill the can three-quarters full with vinegar.

STEP 5

Add several drops of red food coloring.

STEP 6

Add one tablespoon of baking soda and watch out! Your volcano will now erupt.

STEP 7

Keep adding vinegar and baking soda for as long as you'd like to keep your volcano erupting.

Card-Jitsu Fire

TIP

Head outdoors and use dirt or sand instead of clay to form the mountain around the can!

CARD-JITSU

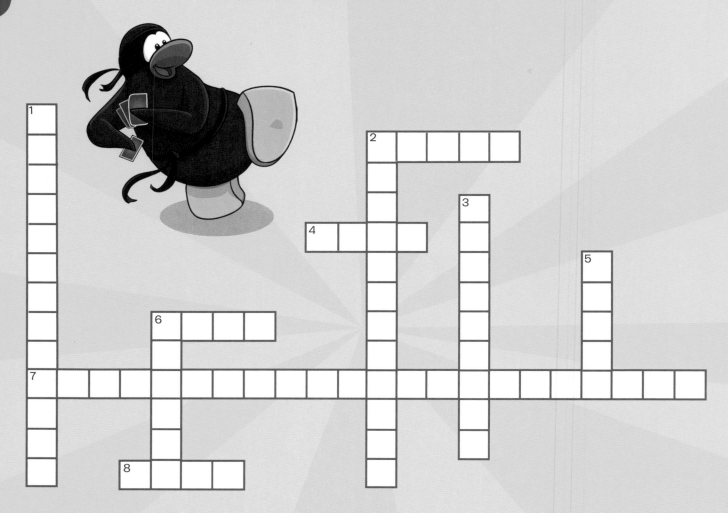

ACROSS

2. Beat Sensei to become this.
4. Aspiring ninjas can train here.
6. Freeze your opponents with this element.
7. Ninjas can buy special gear here.
8. Melt the competition with this element.

DOWN

1. Master *Card-Jitsu* to move on to this game.
2. Only those who defeat Sensei can enter this place.
3. A penguin must have one of these before challenging Sensei.
5. Master this element or you'll get all wet.
6. A wise penguin who teaches others the way of the ninja.

SNOWBALL CUPCAKES

These snowballs look good enough to eat—that's because they are actually cupcakes. Better not get into a snowball fight with these in your living room!

YOU WILL NEED:

- box of white cake mix plus the ingredients listed on the box to make the cupcakes
- mini-muffin pan
- can of vanilla frosting
- 1 bag of sweetened flaked coconut

ASK A PARENT FOR HELP

STEP 1

Follow the directions on the box to make the cupcake batter. Fill mini-muffin pans three-quarters full and bake for twelve to fifteen minutes, until the tops are golden brown and a toothpick inserted in the center of a cupcake comes out clean.

STEP 2

Allow mini cupcakes to cool for about five minutes in the pan. Remove from the pan and let cool completely.

STEP 3

Cut the tops off the cupcakes. Take two cupcake bottoms, spread some frosting on the cut sides, and join together. Frost the two joined cupcake halves all over with frosting. (Warning: This will get a little messy!)

STEP 4

Spread the flaked coconut on a plate. Roll the frosted cupcake in the coconut until completely covered. You've got your own edible snowball!

CARD-JITSU SALAD

Next time you are in the mood to practice your *Card-Jitsu* skills, whip up a tasty fruit or green salad. Instead of cards representing the elements of Snow, Water, and Fire, your salad ingredients will.

With a parent's help, chop up the fruits and vegetables for your salad.

ASK A PARENT FOR HELP

If you're making fruit salad, try using these ingredients to represent the elements:
    Snow: coconut and sliced bananas
    Water: watermelon and blueberries
    Fire: strawberries and raspberries

For a green salad, try using these ingredients:
    Snow: snow peas and iceberg lettuce
    Water: cucumbers and watercress
    Fire: tomatoes and red peppers

TIP

Switch any of the fruits and vegetables suggested here for your favorites.

Top with your favorite salad dressing.

Give yourself and your opponent a plate of salad. Sit across from each other, bow, then close your eyes and stick your fork in your salad. Hold your fork up and open your eyes. Water puts out Fire, Fire melts Snow, and Snow freezes Water. So if you've got a strawberry on your fork and your opponent has a banana, you win the round! Gobble up your forkful and play again.

If you have more than one piece of food on your fork, play the piece that is closest to the end of the fork.

THE HAUNTING OF THE MINE SHACK SILLY STORY

Fill in the blanks with a friend to come up with your own funny Club Penguin tale!

Hint: A **noun** is a person, place, or thing. An **adjective** is a word that describes something. A **verb** is an action word.

Example:

Head over to the ___Gift Shop___ to buy a/an ___silly___ puffle.
NOUN   ADJECTIVE

_____ and _____ were taking a walk through the Mine
YOUR PENGUIN'S NAME   YOUR FRIEND'S PENGUIN'S NAME

Shack. They had heard there was going to be a/an _____ party there, but it was
ADJECTIVE

_____ and _____. There was not a/an _____ to be seen.
ADJECTIVE   ADJECTIVE   ANIMAL

"It looks like the _____ has been canceled," _____ said.
NOUN   YOUR PENGUIN'S NAME

"But I think we're _____!" _____ said. "We already passed
ADJECTIVE   YOUR FRIEND'S PENGUIN'S NAME

that same _____ _____ times!"
NOUN   NUMBER

"There's a door in the wall of the _____," _____ said. "Let's go in there."
NOUN   YOUR PENGUIN'S NAME

They _____ through the _____. Suddenly, the door slammed shut behind
VERB (PAST TENSE)   NOUN

them! It was very _____. Then they heard footsteps.
ADJECTIVE

"My _____ head," a muffled voice moaned. "I can't find my head!"
ADJECTIVE

The door creaked open. A/An _____ _____ shuffled into the room.
ADJECTIVE   NOUN

A _____ liquid oozed from where its head should be.
COLOR

_____ and _____ screamed. They ran past the
YOUR PENGUIN'S NAME   YOUR FRIEND'S PENGUIN'S NAME

_____ and out of the Mine Shack.
NOUN

"Where did they go?" the _____ asked. It poked its head through its
NOUN

_____. It wasn't a/an _____, it was _____!
ARTICLE OF CLOTHING   NOUN   NAME OF CLUB PENGUIN CHARACTER

"I was hoping they'd help me find my _____ head. I was on my way to the party when
ADJECTIVE

I lost part of my _____ costume. And I had brought this _____ beverage,
ADJECTIVE   ADJECTIVE

but it spilled all over me. Oh well. There should be another Club Penguin _____ soon!"
NOUN

MAKE YOUR OWN STALACTITES AND STALAGMITES

The Mine is home to interesting rock formations called stalactites and stalagmites. You can grow your own at home with this cool experiment.

YOU WILL NEED:

- warm water
- large bowl
- Epsom salts (or baking soda)
- two glass jars
- string
- small, metal washers (or paperclips)
- plate

FUN FACT

Stalactites grow on the ceiling of the cave. Stalagmites grow from the ground.

STEP 1

Pour warm water into a large bowl. You can use hot tap water. The amount of water you'll need depends on what size jars you are using. Mix in the Epsom salts or baking soda until it stops dissolving into the water. You're going to want to mix in a lot!

STEP 2

Pour the solution evenly between two glass jars.

STEP 3

Dip the string into the solution until it is completely wet. Tie a washer or attach a paper clip to each end of the string. Insert one end of the string into each of the jars.

STEP 4

Put a small plate between the two jars. There should be a slight dip in the part of the string that is hanging over the plate.

STEP 5

Monitor your jars daily to see if stalactites and stalagmites are forming. Track the changes in your jars in the spaces provided.

DAY 1: _____

DAY 2: _____

DAY 3: _____

DAY 4: _____

DAY 5: _____

DAY 6: _____

DAY 7: _____

TIP

For colorful stalagmites and stalactites, try adding a few drops of food coloring to your salt and water solution.

CLAY TIME!

Never sculpted a penguin before? No problem! Follow these easy steps to make your very own penguin figures out of clay.

YOU WILL NEED:

- clay for the body of the penguin, your choice of color
- yellow clay
- white clay
- black clay
- clay modeling tool or plastic knife

ASK A PARENT FOR HELP

STEP 1

Choose the color clay you would like for the body of your penguin. Roll the clay into a ball.

STEP 2

Roll the ball between your hands to elongate it into a tube shape.

STEP 3

Pinch the clay where the neck of the penguin would be until you have a shape that resembles a bowling pin. Smooth the bottom of the penguin so that it sits flat on the ground.

STEP 4

Take clay the same color as the body and pinch it into two small balls. Roll each ball out, one at a time, to form the arms. Attach to the body.

STEP 5

Take a small amount of yellow clay and roll it into a small, thin oval. This will be your penguin's beak. Attach it to the face of the penguin.

STEP 6

Take a small ball of yellow clay, roll it into a ball, and flatten. With the modeling tool, cut the flattened ball in half and then cut one of the halves in half. Attach these two pieces to the bottom of the penguin. These will be the penguin's feet.

STEP 7

Take a small amount of white clay and roll it into a ball. Flatten it until it is very thin. Cut out the shape of a penguin tummy, and then attach it to the body of your penguin.

STEP 8

Take a small amount of white clay and roll it into a small oval. Cut the clay into the shape of your penguin's eyes.

STEP 9

Attach the eyes to the penguin's face, right above the beak.

STEP 10

Take a small bit of the black clay for the eyeballs of the penguin. Roll into two tiny balls. Attach to the whites of the penguin's eyes.

STEP 11

Take a tiny pinch of black clay and roll it into a long, thin string. This will be your penguin's mouth. Cut to desired length and form into a *U* shape. Place on your penguin's beak.

Hint: If you make a mistake, don't worry! Simply re-roll the clay and start again.

SUSHI SANDWICH ROLLS

Sushi is traditionally made with raw fish, and penguins love it! If you've never tried it before, you can start with these sandwiches made from bread and your favorite fillings.

YOU WILL NEED:

- a rolling pin, if using sandwich bread
- your favorite kind of sandwich bread or wrap (Try a spinach wrap for that seaweed sushi look!)
- your favorite sandwich fixings, like peanut butter and jelly, tuna fish, turkey breast, etc.

ASK A PARENT FOR HELP

STEP 1

If using sandwich bread, use the rolling pin to roll it out gently and make it thinner—but not so thin that it tears!

STEP 2

Spread your ingredients onto the bread or wrap.

STEP 3

Roll from the long end and keep rolling until you have a long tube.

STEP 4

Have a parent use a sharp knife to cut the tube into circles about an inch wide.

STEP 5

Dig in!

FILLING SUGGESTIONS

PEANUT BUTTER SUSHI

Try peanut butter with jelly or sliced bananas

CHEESEBURGER SUSHI

Roast beef, cheese, pickles, ketchup, lettuce, and tomatoes

PIZZA SUSHI

Shredded or diced mozzarella cheese, diced tomatoes, and fresh basil leaves

TUNA SALAD SUSHI

Try your favorite tuna fish recipe with any of the following: lettuce, onions, celery, or bean sprouts

TURKEY SUSHI

Slices of turkey breast are delicious paired with: hummus and cucumber; cheese and mayo; or bacon, lettuce, and tomato

CREAM CHEESE SUSHI

Spread cream cheese on your bread and top with one of the following: jelly, raisins, nuts, pineapple, or cucumber

NAME THAT PLAY

There's a new play at the Stage. To find out what it is, follow the instructions to cross out letters in the grid. The remaining letters will spell out the name of the latest play.

1 Do you know the name of this Stage character? Cross out any letters found in his name.

3 Cross out any letters found in this Stage character's name.

2 Cross out the letters from the first word in this mini-game's name.

4 Cross out any letters left in column 6.

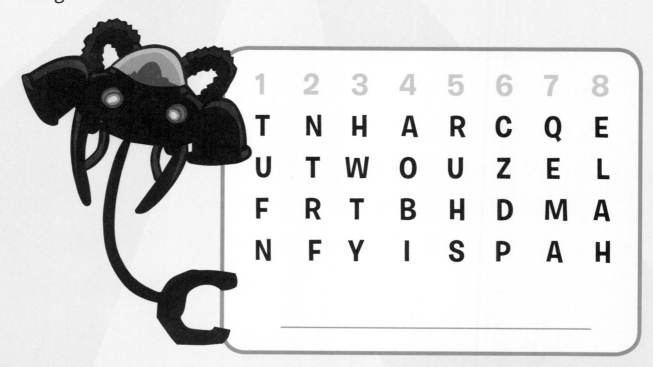

	1	2	3	4	5	6	7	8
	T	N	H	A	R	C	Q	E
	U	T	W	O	U	Z	E	L
	F	R	T	B	H	D	M	A
	N	F	Y	I	S	P	A	H

_____

WHO SAID IT?

Do you remember your favorite Club Penguin plays? Put your memory—and your friends—to the test with this game!

Write down some lines from Club Penguin plays on separate strips of papers. Have your friends take turns reading the lines. Everyone else has to guess the name of the play and the character who said them. Here are a few suggestions to get you started:

 "Once upon a time, a princess dressed all in red . . ." Twee, *Fairy Fables*

 "Is it too late for a swimming lesson? I wish I'd brought my water wings!" Daring Daisy, *Underwater Adventure*

 "Last time I buy a time machine for ten coins . . ." Chester, *The Penguin That Time Forgot*

 "As long as the ghost is ghosting, I will not sing!" Helga, *Haunting of the Viking Opera*

 "Can't find rare puffles without a little danger!" Alaska, *Quest for the Golden Puffle*

 "Lead the way, Funny Pig!" Monkey King, *Secrets of the Bamboo Forest*

 "Something fishy this way comes." Countess, *The Twelfth Fish*

 "Another day, another crime solved." Jacque Hammer, *Ruby and the Ruby*

 "Ensign, increase emergency power!" Captain Snow, *Space Adventure*

 "With great power comes great hunger." Shadow Guy, *Squidzoid vs. Shadow Guy and Gamma Gal*

TIP

You can play this game with lines from your favorite TV shows, movies, and songs, too!

IMPROV ACTING GAME

Improv, or improvisational, acting is when actors use audience suggestions to create a scene on the spot. There is no script and no rehearsal! The results are usually very funny! Here's how to ham it up with your friends.

PLACES, EVERYONE!

Actors need an audience! If you've got four or more friends together, take turns. Or ask some family members to be the audience. Ask the audience members who the actors should play (penguin), where they should be (place), and what they should be doing (activity).

If you've only got two people playing, write out these suggestions on strips of paper. Put all the penguin strips of paper in a bag labeled PENGUIN, the place strips in a bag labeled PLACE, and the activity strips in a bag labeled ACTIVITY. Have each actor pick from the PENGUIN bag, then pick only one strip from the PLACE and ACTIVITY bags. Now start acting!

Keep going until you run out of new ideas for the scene. Then pick a new penguin/place/activity.

PENGUIN

Captain Rockhopper
Wizard
Sensei
Pop Star
Cadence
Chef
Aunt Arctic
Movie Star
Gary the Gadget Guy
Superhero

PLACE

Zoo
Jungle
Pirate Ship
Beach
Amusement Park
School
Restaurant
Rock Concert
Toy Store
Summer Camp

ACTIVITY

Searching for buried treasure
Running a race
Fishing
Building a time machine
Walking the red carpet at a movie premiere
Running from a monster
Inventing a new dance
Filming an action/adventure movie
Competing in a cooking competition show
Flying an airplane

PENGUIN ACTORS LOGIC PUZZLE

These six penguins are about to put on the play *Norman Swarm Has Been Transformed*. Can you figure out which penguin is playing which part? Carefully read the clues below to find out!

1 The orange penguin's character can't fly.

2 The aqua penguin's character is NOT a bug.

3 Both the pink and black penguins' characters can fly.

4 The peach penguin is playing the part of a slow-moving mollusk.

5 The name of the black penguin's part rhymes with *buzz*.

6 The green penguin is playing the title role.

	NORMAN SWARM	BONNIE THE MOTH	GLADYS THE SPIDER	BERNARD THE GARDEN GNOME	TONI THE SNAIL	FUZZ THE BEE
PINK PENGUIN						
ORANGE PENGUIN						
GREEN PENGUIN						
BLACK PENGUIN						
AQUA PENGUIN						
PEACH PENGUIN						

HERBERT P. BEAR'S SEAWEED SMOOTHIE

What is Herbert up to when he isn't working on his next dastardly plan? This vegetarian villain likes to come up with new recipes. And the one that sounds the scariest is his "seaweed smoothie." Whip up a batch, then ask your friends and family if they dare you to drink it. Only you—and those brave enough to try it—will learn its true secret: It's delicious!

ASK A PARENT FOR HELP

YOU WILL NEED:

- 1 cup spinach (this is your "seaweed")
- 1 ripe banana
- 1 cup cubed pineapple
- ½ cup pineapple juice
- ice cubes, about ½ cup

Put all the ingredients in a blender and blend until smooth. Make sure to ask an adult for permission before using the blender, and make sure the cover is on before you blend. Otherwise, you'll have a seaweed mess!

TIP

For an even sweeter smoothie, make your ice cubes out of pineapple juice or your favorite fruit juice!

HUNGRY PUFFLE

Puffles need to be fed and cared for. But only one of these puffles is hungry and ready to dive into a yummy box of Puffle-Os. Can you help the hungry puffle get to the food?

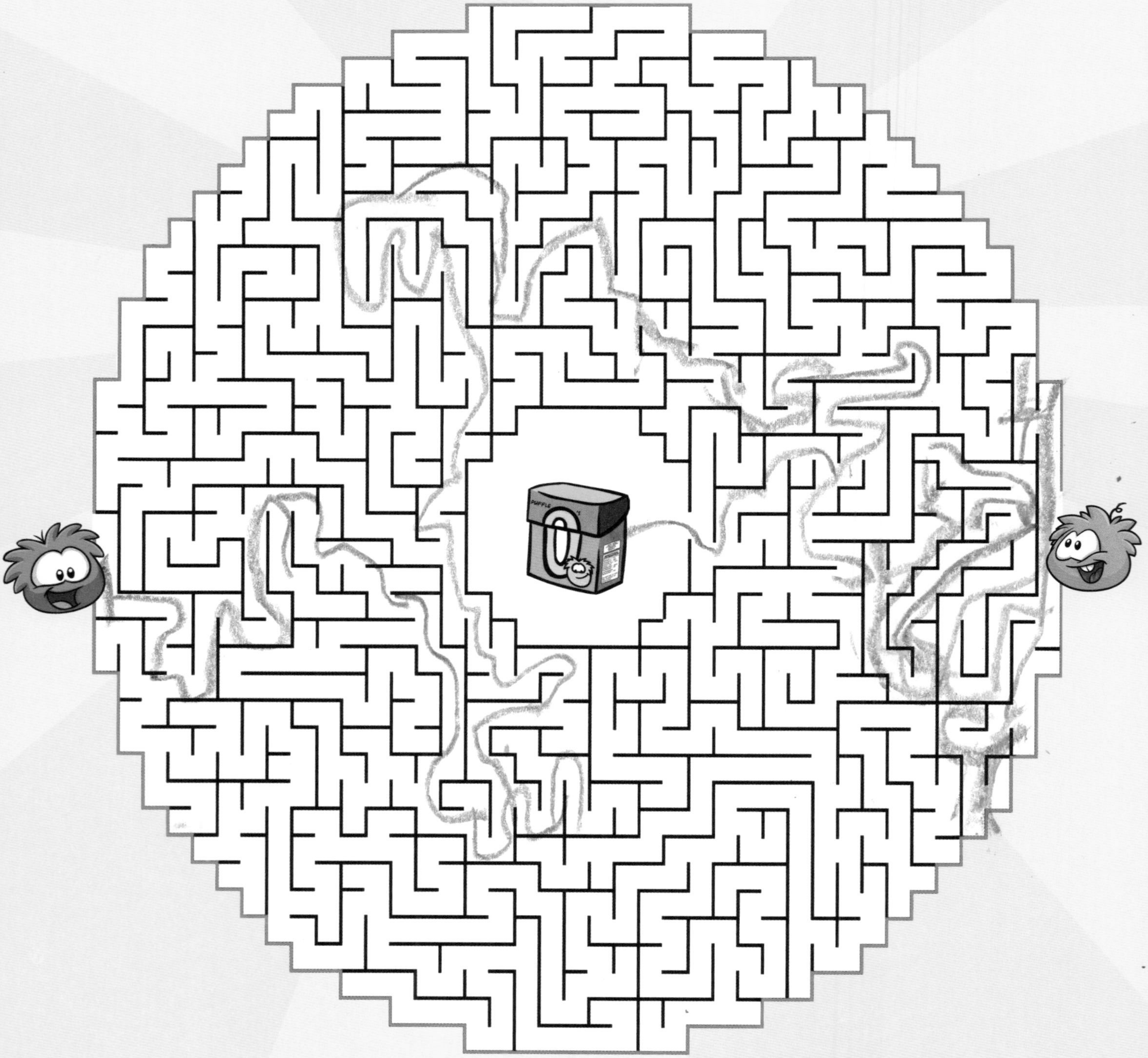

PUFFLES ON A LOG

How many puffles can fit on a log? Find out when you make this quick and easy snack.

YOU WILL NEED:

- 1 banana, peeled
- peanut butter
- candy-coated chocolate candies in different colors

ASK A PARENT FOR HELP

Put the banana on a plate. Spread peanut butter over the banana. Sprinkle with the candies and enjoy!

PARTY LIKE A PUFFLE

There are nine types of puffles and each color has a different personality. The next time you throw a bash, get your theme inspiration from a puffle!

BLUE: FRIENDSHIP PARTY

Celebrate your friends with fun activities you can all do together, such as making friendship bracelets or creating a friendship chain out of construction paper. Have everyone write their name on a strip before linking the pieces together.

RED: ADVENTURE PARTY

Let the adventure begin with a fun treasure or scavenger hunt-themed party. Check out the tips on how to make your own treasure hunt on page 26.

PINK: ULTIMATE SPORTS FAN PARTY

Host your own sports fan party by giving your guests a chance to compete in a series of races and events like hula-hooping and beanbag tosses.

BLACK: SKATEBOARD PARTY

Gather your friends and compare your skateboard skills. Can you balance on two wheels or take a sharp turn?

TIP

Try mixing party themes to come up with your own unique party creation.

GREEN: COMEDY PARTY

Bring on the funny with a comedy-themed party. Rent your favorite funny movies, and write jokes on slips of paper, put them in a bowl, and have each guest pick one and read it aloud.

PURPLE: DANCE PARTY

Limbo, freeze dance, and musical chairs (even musical sleeping bags if you're having a sleepover party!) can all be a part of your dance party.

YELLOW: CRAFT PARTY

Tell your friends to bring a smock and you'll supply the paints, markers, paper, glue, and other items for a craft party.

WHITE: WINTER PARTY

Celebrate the snowy season with a winter party. Ask your guests to dress all in white, replace the potato with a snowball made out of Styrofoam for a game of Hot Potato, and play Pin the Carrot on the Snowman.

ORANGE: WACKY PARTY

Invite your friends to come wearing the craziest clothes they own, and suggest they wear their clothes backward or inside out. Hide some whoopee cushions around your house and turn objects upside down or sideways (with your parent's permission) for a truly wacky party.

TIME TO DECORATE!
SPOT THE DIFFERENCES

It's party time! These penguins are helping to decorate a tree house in the Forest for the latest Club Penguin bash. Thirteen things have been changed in the bottom picture. See if you can find and circle all the differences.

CLUB PENGUIN PARTIES

Penguins love to party! About once a month, Club Penguin throws an island-wide party. Search for some of the most memorable bashes in this word puzzle. Remember to search backward, forward, and diagonally.

```
E A A Y Y T A L L N Z I A M Y N P
W T A P I A F A E K N I U E R V Z
E D H L R F D E U G E S N D A N E
S K F G W I W I L Z I Q H I S F Q
S A K E I O L G L C I S Q E R Y C
E H I M L L W F J O D D Y V E E V
K A P L I S F A O C H S E A V L T
H K A Q G N M F Q O D B J L I F S
R H N T K G E E O C L I P A N F O
J F E I Q X X B A L M S R Q N U T
A D V E N T U R E C A H D M A P B
M R Q B I Q I O K B Q V M A F W S
G X D E I S W P J X T C I Z Y T N
F A I R E C U P Y H A Q X T K Z D
L W Q H X E V R D I U O H P S E D
S D R A W A Y A L P N I U G N E P
Y A D H T R A E S I D Y J I S Z F
```

WORD BANK

MEDIEVAL

FESTIVAL OF FLIGHT

PENGUIN PLAY AWARDS

HALLOWEEN

ADVENTURE

PUFFLE

MUSIC JAM

APRIL FOOL'S DAY

EARTH DAY

HOLIDAY

FAIR

ANNIVERSARY

HIDDEN PINS

A new pin is hidden on the island every two weeks. If you find it, you can use it to decorate your player card! Two pins are hiding in this puzzle. To find them, cross out the letters found in the word *igloos* every time you see them. Write down the extra letters in the order they appear on the lines below.

```
I G L O O S I G L O O S C I G
L O O S U I G L O O S P C I G
L O O S A I G L O O S K I G L
O O S I G L O O S I G L O O S
I G L O O S E I G L O O S I G
L O O S I G L O O S R I G L O
O O S U I G L O O S B I G L O
O S I G L O O S I G L O O S Y
```

_ _ _ _ _ _ _ and _ _ _ _

CLUB PENGUIN MAGNET

Take your penguin player card off-line and put it on the coolest place in your house—your refrigerator!

YOU WILL NEED:

- craft sticks
- paints
- one of the player card backgrounds from page 61
- glue
- markers
- magnets
- optional: stickers and glitter for decorating your frame

ASK A PARENT FOR HELP

STEP 1

The craft sticks will be the frame for your player card background. Take two craft sticks and glue them together side by side (NOT on top of each other). Repeat with the remaining sticks until you are left with four separate pieces. These will form your frame.

STEP 2

Assemble your frame. Place one piece on the left and one piece on the right. The two remaining pieces will go along the top and bottom, resting on top of the left and right pieces. Glue the top and bottom pieces onto the left and right pieces.

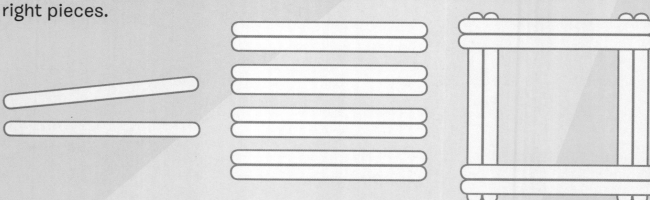

STEP 3

Cut out the player card background of your choice. Put yourself into the picture! Glue or tape a photograph of yourself onto the background, or draw a picture of yourself or your penguin on a separate piece of paper, cut out, and glue or tape to the background.

STEP 4

Adjust the frame pieces until your background is centered.

STEP 5

Tape the player card background onto the back of the frame.

STEP 6

One the glue has dried, you can now decorate your frame. (See decorating tips below.)

STEP 7

Glue magnets onto the back of the frame, on both the left and right sides. Let the glue dry. Then hang.

DECORATING TIPS

Design your background like a real player card. Paint the craft sticks blue and paint or write your penguin name across the top. Get creative—anything goes when it comes to expressing your Club Penguin style!

ANSWER KEY

Page 6
WHO'S APPEARING ON CLUB PENGUIN?
Sensei

Page 7
NAME THAT PLACE

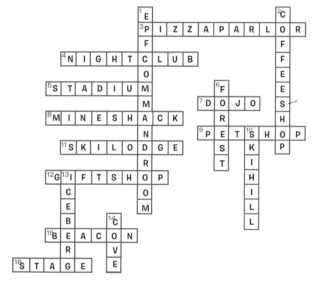

Page 11
PIZZA PARLOR LOGIC PUZZLE
Blue penguin=Hot shrimp pizza

Yellow penguin=Spicy seaweed pizza

Brown penguin=Cheese pizza

Green penguin=Chocolate sprinkle pizza

Red penguin=Marshmallow pizza

Page 16
GARY THE GADGET GUY'S WORD SCRAMBLE
Snowball-Powered Clock

Life Preserver Shooter

Recycletron 3000

Spy Phone

Flare Flinger 3000

Furensic Analyzer 3000

Ski Lift

Cloud Maker 3000

Jet Pack Adventure

Elite Penguin Force

Page 18
PENGUIN, PLACE, OR THING?
The Club Penguin Times

Pages 20-21
FOR YOUR EYES ONLY! SPOT THE DIFFERENCES

ANSWER KEY

Pages 22–23
FAVORITE THINGS

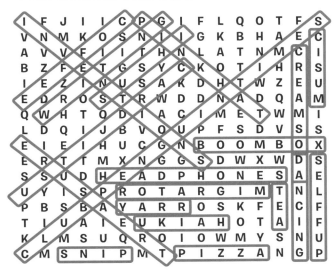

Aunt Arctic:

Club Penguin Times, Pink hat, Puffles, Writing

Cadence:

Boom box, Dancing, Headphones, Music

Captain Rockhopper:

Cream soda, Migrator, Treasure, Yarr

Gary the Gadget Guy:

Coffee, Inventions, Pins, Pizza

Sensei:

Card-Jitsu, Haiku, Sushi, Tea

Page 29
BLACK BELT

Page 32
CARD-JITSU

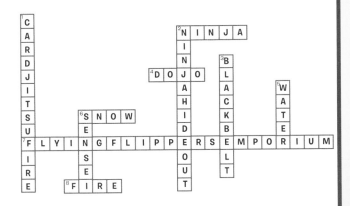

ANSWER KEY

Page 42
NAME THAT PLAY
The Twelfth Fish

Page 46
PENGUIN ACTORS LOGIC PUZZLE

Pink penguin=Bonnie the Moth

Orange penguin=Gladys the Spider

Green penguin=Norman Swarm

Black penguin=Fuzz the Bee

Aqua penguin=Bernard the Garden Gnome

Peach penguin=Toni the Snail

Page 48
HUNGRY PUFFLE

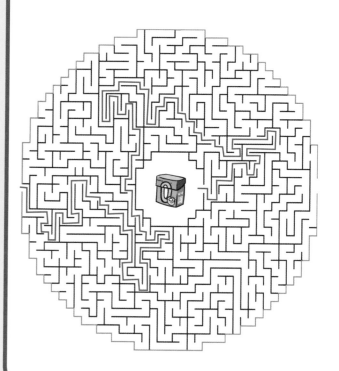

Pages 52-53
TIME TO DECORATE! SPOT THE DIFFERENCES

Page 54
CLUB PENGUIN PARTIES

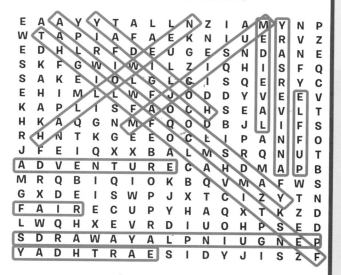

Page 55
HIDDEN PINS

Cupcake and Ruby

PLAYER CARDS

PLAYER CARDS

ICE FISHING PIECES

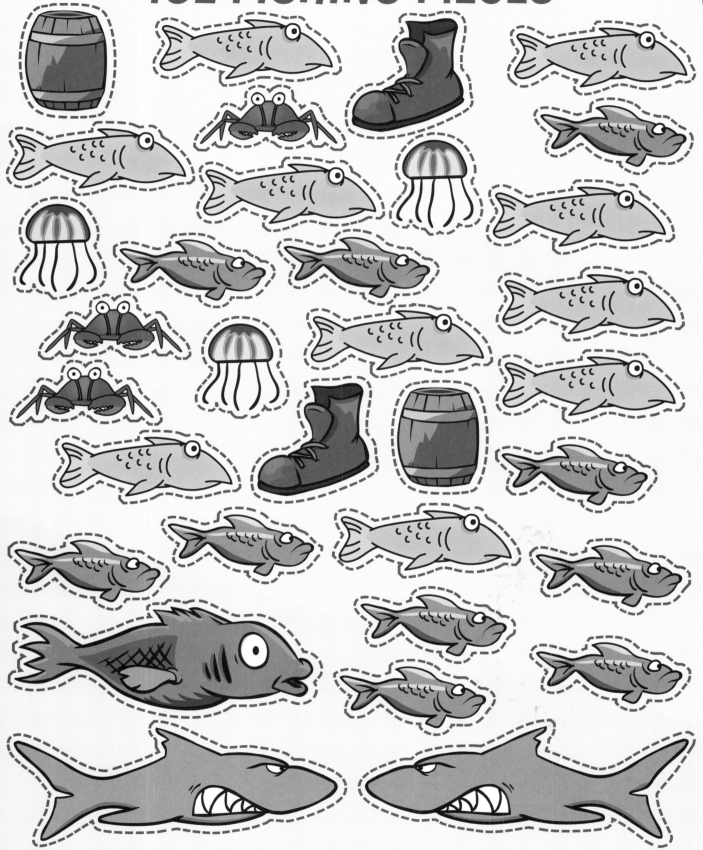

ICE FISHING PIECES

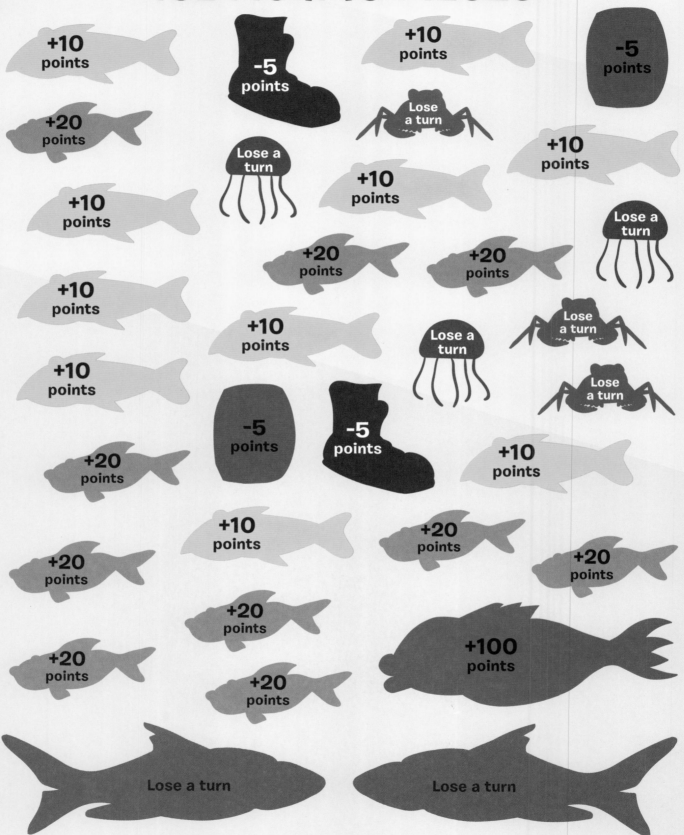